Harcourt Brace & Company

SAN DIEGO NEW YORK LONDON

MY BLUE BOAT

Chris L. Demarest

Library of Congress Cataloging-in-Publication Data
Demarest, Chris L.
My blue boat/Chris L. Demarest.—1st ed.
p. cm.
Summary: While playing with a blue boat in the bath-
tub, a young girl imagines she is on an ocean voyage.
ISBN 0-15-200177-8
[1. Boats and boating—Fiction. 2. Imagination—Fiction.
3. Baths—Fiction.] I. Title.
PZ7.D3914My 1995
[E]—dc20 94-10924

Printed in Singapore

First edition

A B C D E

The illustrations in this book were done in
watercolor and india ink on watercolor paper.
The display and text type were set in Kennerly
by Thompson Type, San Diego, California.
Color separations by Bright Arts, Ltd., Singapore
Printed and bound by Tien Wah Press, Singapore
This book was printed with soya-based inks on
Leykam recycled paper, which contains more than
20 percent postconsumer waste and has a total
recycled content of at least 50 percent.
Production supervision by Warren Wallerstein
and David Hough
Designed by Kaelin Chappell

To Bill and Margaret

My blue boat

catches the wind.

I sail past the sleeping town,

through the channel,

and into the busy harbor.

"Good morning," I call
to the fishing fleet.

My blue boat sails up

and down the swells

and across the wide ocean.

I dance with whales,

play tag with dolphins,

and steer through storms.

My blue boat dips under the moon

as I look for stars

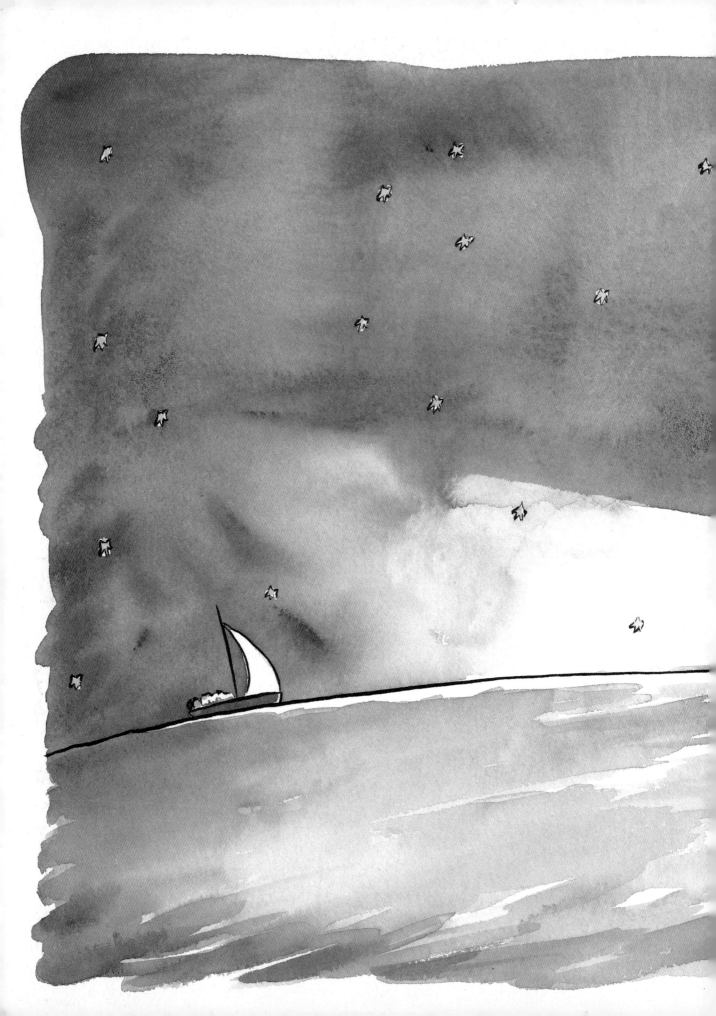

and drift back toward the beacon...

and home.